Loki & Alex

THE ADVENTURES OF A DOG AND HIS BEST FRIEND

CHARLES R. SMITH JR.

Dutton Children's Books • New York

To Adrian and Sabine and their future four-legged friends

——■——

Completing the task of photographing a boy and a dog was not
an easy one. But with the help of several people,
the task became manageable.

A big thanks to Susan Nowak and the ever-energetic
Gandolph for giving the book life. I also owe a big thanks to the
Pinkney family and Rashad for all their help. And lest I forget,
thanks to Jane and Jesse for introducing me to the furry
little mischievous one in the first place— Loki.

Copyright © 2001 by Charles R. Smith Jr.

All rights reserved.

CIP Data is available.

Published in the United States 2001 by Dutton Children's Books,

a division of Penguin Putnam Books for Young Readers

345 Hudson Street, New York, New York 10014

www.penguinputnam.com

Designed by Ellen M. Lucaire

Printed in China

First Edition

1 3 5 7 9 10 8 6 4 2

ISBN 0-525-46700-9

Loki & ALEX

My name is Alex. I'm going to tell you about my dog, Loki, and Loki is going to tell you about me. (By the way, his name is pronounced *low*-key, not *lock*-ee like my sister says.)

I learned that dogs see the world a little differently than people do. Dogs can't see colors quite the same way as humans. So everything Loki sees in the story is in **black** and white, and everything I see is in color.

Since Loki is my best friend, I know lots of things about him. I can always tell what he's thinking, especially when we play. And I know just what makes him happy. See for yourself.

This is my best friend, Loki.
Bark "Hello," Loki.

 This is Alex, my best friend in the whole world.
Boys can't bark. Wave "Hello," Alex.

 Loki can be a very naughty dog.
He sticks his nose where it doesn't belong.

 Alex loves it when I dig out my own treats. Look how happy it makes him!

 Before we play, Loki waits patiently while I take his leash off.

 Hurry up, Alex. I can't sit here all day. Release the hound!

 Loki likes to play follow the leader at the playground.

I gotta keep my nose on Alex so he stays out of trouble.

 Sometimes I'm extra nice to Loki and let him go down the slide.

 HELLLLLPPPP MEEEEEE, ALEXXXX!

I'd take Loki on the jungle gym, too, but I don't think he'd like it.

 Lemme climb up there, Alex. No fair.
I wanna hang upside down, too!

 Loki growls when we play tug-of-war,
but he's just kidding around.

Gimme that rope... Gimme. Mine, mine, MINE!
I'll show YOU whose rope this is!

Here, Loki. Fetch!

 No treat, no fetch. Alex never learns. Why doesn't he toss me a treat instead of a stupid ball?

 Loki loves to have his tummy rubbed. See how he smiles?

Oh no, not The Hand! Alex, stop!! That tickles! Ha-ha-ha-ha-he-he-he!!! Alex, stop!

Running up the steps is part of Loki's workout.

Let's go, Alex! Move those two little legs of yours. Last one up is a fat fur ball.

 After a hard workout, Loki gets a squeeze of water.

 How am I supposed to drink from this thing?
I want my water bowl!

When Loki runs far away in the park, I blow his dog whistle really hard to make sure he can hear it.

 Yikes, that is loud!! YOU'RE HURTING MY EARS, ALEX!

Come on, Loki! Come on, boy! Let's go home.

 Alex, wait! Aren't you forgetting something? Haven't I been good? Haven't I, old buddy, old pal?

 Since Loki was a good dog today, I'm making him jump for a nice big treat.

 Finally... TREATS! Come on, Alex, don't tease a poor pup. I fetched, I ran, I jumped—gimme MY treat!

Ahhh, this is the best treat of all!!

Ahhh, this is the best treat of all!!